CU00842986

QUENTIN JAMES ADVENTURES:

QUENTIN JAMES and the UNDERCOVER AGENT
QUENTIN JAMES and the LOCH of ARTHUR
QUENTIN JAMES and the JACOBITE GOLD
QUENTIN JAMES and the GLOBAL WAR GAMES
QUENTIN JAMES and the ARCTIC ADVENTURE

CYBER SLEUTHS
Bug Wars/Zombie Wars
A Quentin James companion adventure

QUENTIN JAMES and the BATTLE for EDGEWATER
QUENTIN JAMES'S FIFTH YEAR at EDGEWATER

*

THE PRINCE OF LIGHT:
WITCHES" EYE
CASTLE ADVENTUROUS
THE QUEEN OF MAGIC

*

EBENEZER

*

THE LIBRARY
THE LIBRARY: Augustus.

*

THE O'BRIEN DETECTIVE AGENCY

*

UNREQUITED

BASED UPON THE CHARLES DICKENS NOVELLA:

A CHRISTMAS CAROL

CHAPTER ONE

CHRISTMAS EVE

Ebenezer strode out of the Grand Hall unaffected by the cold that steamed his breath or the fog that had settled across the city. He was winter incarnate. The pale blue of his eyes were like ice, his hair, white as the driven snow, fell to his shoulders, his face and frame gaunt, drawn, and skeletal like the trees devoid of leaves. For all these features, it was his voice that put the chill into people's hearts and icy shivers down their spines. Devoid of humanity, it was said.

Placing his tall hat upon his head, he walked down the path cordoned off just for him.

A gust of wind inexplicably struck up and swirled around him, creeping inside his coat, cold, so cold; it stopped him in his tracks.

Ebenezer uncharacteristically shivered and pulled his overcoat together.

The bust of his old friend Jacob Marley caught his eye, the street lamp, and the fog combining to cast it in a sickly yellow light. As the wind howled and moaned, Jacob's features appeared to contort and move as if the sounds were coming from its very mouth; even his thin wispy hair stirred restlessly. All but the eyes, they had not moved at all, yet seemed to hold such horror; Ebenezer felt his skin crawl and blood curdle.

A single word carried on the wind.

"Ebenezerrrrrrrrr."

Ebenezer shook himself of such fanciful thoughts and walked towards his car.

Jacob was dead. He knew this to be true; he had buried him. Not that he could spare the time. It was expected they said, demanded even. Why was everyone so demanding of his time? Jacob was dead, and that was that.

Even though it was a little past three o'clock in the afternoon, it was already dark. The lights in the nearby offices were barely visible through the dense fog that hung thick and heavy in the air. As Ebenezer walked towards his car he thought he could see shadows of people appearing and disappearing within the fog and hear pleading cries of tortured souls carried on the wind as it blew stronger and stronger, raging against him as if whipped into a frenzy by unseen means.

Yet the fog continued to ebb and shift sluggishly, unaffected by this sudden gale.

Ebenezer looked for a logical source, but there was no one along the rope line, no one calling his name, pleading or crying out, no jostling to take his photograph or hand him a gift. In fact, other than himself and his security, there was no one else in sight, which was normally just how he liked it.

Ebenezer loved his job, loved that the common man was held at arm's length. Nobody stopped him in the street to exchange banalities, no one got in his way as his long stride carried him quickly along, no one begged him for money or asked him the time, even the dogs on their leash sensed to give him a wide berth, their wagging tails drooping until he had passed. He revelled in that sense of power; of the self-worth, it gave him. He was a man of stature, of presence and he had no time for any that were not. Nevertheless, just for a moment, he felt the loneliness of his existence as the fog closed about him, its ice-cold tendrils upon his face felt as if the fingers of the ghostly apparitions were touching him.

The wind dropped as suddenly as it started.

He shivered again.

The noise of horses' hooves clattering on the cobbled streets drew him to the road. The sound rose yet its origin remained hidden by the fog until, at the last moment, an old carriage hearse, drawn by six black horses, burst forth, forcing Ebenezer to step backwards as it tore past as if the very hounds of hell were chasing it. He watched as the fog swallowed it whole, not only removing it from sight but also sound. The utter silence that followed, unnerving. He looked around at his security guards, expecting astonishment, amazement, alarmed for his personal safety but they were just standing there looking alert but immobile.

'Bah,' he said to no one in particular. 'Damn head cold.'

Climbing into his car, he immediately lowered the divide between him and his driver. He could feel the scant warmth of the heater, kept at its lowest, warming the air. If he had his way, the heater would have been removed. The chill would keep his driver more alert, more attentive to his duties but he had been persuaded otherwise. A moment of weakness he prodded at like a bruise whenever he got into the car. His mouth, usually a thin straight firm line, curled into a scowl as he dwelt on it.

Before the door was closed for him, a cheery voice called out, 'A Merry Christmas, Uncle!' And a young man dived into the car to sit alongside him.

Ebenezer's scowl deepened as he made a mental note to reprimand his security. No one should be allowed to dive into his car, not murderer, terrorist, mugger, or nephew!

To distract himself, to gain a moment to gather his wits so scattered at this sudden intrusion, he unwrapped one of his favourite sweets.

'Bah!' he said and offered his nephew the bowl. Never let it be said he was not a well-mannered man.

'Humbug!'

His Nephew laughed.

'Offering me one of your precious mints, Uncle? You don't mean that I am sure.'

Ebenezer's brow furrowed, his eyebrows bristled.

'I do, take one or be done with it. Merry Christmas is it? What have you to be so merry about? Won the lottery, got a pay rise, or improved your lot somehow?'

The nephew laughed.

'Oh, Uncle, money is not everything, for if it were you would be the happiest man alive but instead, you are miserable despite your money and power.'

'Bah,' Ebenezer said again. 'Humbug?' he offered again, having no answer to his nephew's argument.

'Now don't be cross, Uncle, it's Christmas after all,' the nephew said placatingly.

The frown deepened even further.

'What else can I be? Look at the world we live in. Merry Christmas? It's just an excuse for more fools to spend money they do not have, on things they do not need instead of paying their bills, paying their taxes, and saving for their retirement. An aging population is getting older by another year whilst the country they look to support them is getting poorer. If I had my will,' said Ebenezer, building up a head of steam as he vented out his frustrations, 'every idiot that say's Merry Christmas would be fined. That would put a few pounds back into social security to supplement their wastrel ways.'

'Uncle,' the Nephew pleaded, 'calm down. You'll have a stroke or a heart attack or something. Surely Christmas is a time for putting aside such worries.'

'Nephew!' barked Ebenezer. 'Keep Christmas your delusional, self-serving way and I will keep mine, leading by example and doing without the frivolities, thank you very much.'

'But that is my point, Uncle, you don't keep it, not in practice, not in your heart,' said the nephew, trying to make him see.

'Then leave me to it, Nephew. Do I jump in your car preaching my thoughts on how you live your life, spend your Christmas, much good it would do you? No! So leave me to mine.'

'Whilst I do many things, many deeds simply for the pleasure of the good I feel rather than any profit I forgo, Christmas amongst them, I do feel Christmas is a special time. A time for having fun, being kind, forgiving those acts that have aggrieved me during the year; a time for charity and goodwill; a time, the only time perhaps, where *every* man and woman see's those less fortunate than themselves and does what little they can to help. So whilst it may not fill my pockets with gold, it certainly fills my heart with joy and for that I say, God bless it.'

The driver in the front applauded without thinking and, coming to the sudden realisation of his act, froze mid clap before looking straight ahead, turning down the heater in appeasement.

Ebenezer turned on his driver. Finally, someone he could take out his ire on.

'One more show of insubordination like that and you will spend Christmas standing in the unemployment lines.'

Turning to his nephew.

'You speak with passion. You're a natural orator, my lad, you should have followed my footsteps into politics, like I always said.'

'That was never my desire, Uncle,' he held his hands up in surrender. 'Now stop being angry with me. Come; say you will join us tomorrow for dinner.'

Ebenezer shook his head. 'No, Nephew I cannot,'

'But why, Uncle, please tell me why?'

'Tell me why you married that pauper girl?'

'Because I love her.'

'Love! You married for love! That is more ridiculous than saying a Merry Christmas. Get out of my car! Good afternoon, Nephew!'

'I am not asking you for anything, I need neither favours nor money, why can't we be family, Uncle, friends even?'

'I said good afternoon, Nephew.'

'Uncle I feel sorry for you, to find you so guarded, so hard. We have never argued, never fallen out, or had a cross word, so in keeping with the season and holding onto my Christmas joy and pleasure I wish you, with all my heart, a Merry Christmas.'

Ebenezer looked out of the window, unable to look his Nephew in the eye and maintain his temper. The boy was a fool, and there was no reasoning with fools, as well he knew.

'Good afternoon!' he yelled.

'And a Happy New Year!' The nephew retorted, getting out of the car.

'Merry Christmas, Sir,' called the driver, risking the ire of his boss but moved by the passion of this young man.

'That's the spirit, Bob, Merry Christmas,' the nephew called back.

The door slammed.

'Back to the office,' Ebenezer snapped curtly, as he settled back into the plush leather seats.

The car pulled away smoothly, their journey unhindered by traffic, his security clearing the way ahead.

'Humbug,' he said, reaching for another mint.

*

Ebenezer stepped out of the car.

'I suppose you will be wanting tomorrow off?'

'If convenient, Sir?'

'Convenient? Convenient? Of course it's not convenient. Supposed I wish to go out somewhere, what do I do then? No, Sir, it is not convenient nor fair. I can be called upon tonight, tomorrow, *and* the next day and yet you would consider yourself hard done by if I were to call you in or dock you a day's pay I'll be bound?'

The driver smiled hesitantly. 'It is only once a year, Sir.'

'Well if you must you must, but be all the earlier the following day.'

'Yes, Sir, thank you, Sir.'

The chauffeur dashed off before his boss had a change of heart and to get home where his children were waiting to play the games he had promised before leaving for work that morning.

CHAPTER TWO

ORPHANAGES AND SHELTERS

As Ebenezer strode down the corridors towards his office, he groaned. *What do they want now*? Why was everyone so demanding of his time?

Up ahead were two portly gentlemen both holding books and folders.

'Matthews, Brown, what can I do for you two gentlemen, as if I didn't know?' Ebenezer said, sweeping past them into his office.

'Sir, we are seeking funds to help those less fortunate than ourselves this festive season. The poor, the homeless,' said the first man.

'And the Orphans, Sir, both here and abroad,' added the second. 'They suffer so greatly at this time of the year. Tens of thousands in this country alone are in want of the basic necessities, hundreds of thousands across the world; I am sure you would agree.'

Ebenezer, having only just sat down behind his desk, stood up again, clearly vexed.

'Have we not sent monies to create refugee camps, schools, and hospitals abroad?'

'We have sent millions indeed, Sir, though I wish it were not necessary,' replied the first portly gentleman.

'There we are in agreement. Have we not set up the factories and shelters for the unemployed to work and the homeless to sleep? Orphanages and homes for the children to have a roof over their heads and a bed to sleep in across this great country of ours? Are they not full and productive?'

'Indeed, Sir, all are full and productive.'

Ebenezer sat down. 'For a minute I thought something had gone awry, our policies deviated, our good works undone.'

The two gentlemen looked at each other.

'Sir, there are many who cannot find work in the factories or a bed in the shelters,' said the first man.

'There are many children who won't have presents to open, toys to play with in the morning, Sir, or have treats to eat,' added the second.

Ebenezer sat behind his desk and placed his head in his hands. 'You talk of treats and toys? Men and women too lazy to find work and you ask me for more money. Nobody asks me what I want, have you noticed that? Everyone comes to me and asks for something, money for this cause or that crusade, all very worthy, all very good causes, but nobody asks me what I want.'

The two gentlemen looked at each other.

'And what is it you want, Sir?'

'I want to be left alone; to have one night where I am not hounded by men like you, wanting more, always more. We cannot afford to keep the idle merry and the old people warm in their own homes. We have created the group homes, shelters, workhouses, orphanages and those in need must go there. And don't read me letters from early twenty something's moaning they cannot afford homes of their own. Why should the Government give them homes? They should live with their parents; get jobs, save their money as we had to. Nowadays the young have their hands out, looking for everything to be given to them, without the work, effort and sacrifice we all made to buy those same things. They have no appreciation of what they have and what it takes to earn them.'

'It's a different time, Sir.'

'A different time? BAH! They borrow beyond their means and cannot pay it back. And who do they blame? ME! As if I forced their hands to sign the agreements, to take the money, and spend it on what? Holidays, games consoles, new cars, and bigger houses. BAH, I say! If it wasn't for their wastrel ways I would not have had to spend money building the Debtor's Prisons to house those wastrels.'

'Many would rather die than go to those places, Sir.'

Ebenezer shrugged. 'A noble sacrifice and one I would honour, now if you want me to find funds for cremations and burials I am willing to listen. You know my position on this, the planet cannot sustain us all indefinitely, if these people would rather die, then let them get on with it and decrease the surface population. You, Mr Matthews are the Minister for Housing. You, Mr Brown, the Minister for Employment, the specifics are yours to resolve, this is not my business. Wasn't it the Leader of the Opposition that said; "it is enough for each of us to attend to his or her business and not interfere with other peoples," when I tried to intervene personally on a matter in his party? I think it was.

Good afternoon, gentlemen.'

The two gentlemen turned and left, not daring to voice anymore arguments or dissatisfaction.

*

The Prime Minister worked through his correspondence, returning phone calls, sending out emails and as he worked, his temper eased and his mood improved. Work was where he found his peace, his calm and he worked diligently long into the night.

CHAPTER THREE

A VOICE FROM THE PAST

The sound of the old church bells striking the hour was an eerie counterpoint to the dark night and thick fog that sat over the city, swirling and eddying restlessly. The temperature had dropped further and was so icy cold people walked along the streets, wrapped up so tight, only their eyes were visible. Down Oxford Street, the kids darted here and there only stopping to stare into the brightly lit and colourful shop fronts of the toy, sweet, and cake shops, all decorated with festive cheer, as their parents did their last minute shopping. On many corners, men gathered around braziers which burned with a crackle and pop, trying to warm their chilled hands and faces.

*

Ebenezer decided he had finished for the day and pulled on his jacket. The faint sounds of carol singers floating in the air sent a surge of hot anger through his body. He had forbidden the practice

23

of singers in the lobby with their copper bowls taking the odd coin or two from his workers who would then complain about poor wages. He stormed out of his office as the singers struck up another song

'Silent Night...'

Ebenezer saw one his senior advisors and beckoned him over.

'Clear these kids out of here; you know my thoughts on this.'

'Yes, Sir.'

Nothing needed to be said however. The kids, seeing him approach, the scowl across his face sending shivers down their spines were packing up and fleeing in fear, before any instructions were issued.

Ebenezer continued on to the kitchens. There were formal dining rooms of course or he could have had food sent to his private quarters, but he preferred to eat in the kitchens, to read the papers and review the budget forecasts.

'Another slice of bread please, Mrs Poulter,' he asked his housekeeper, as he sipped the thin broth.

'Yes, Sir, it will be a moment, I need to pop to the larder and get a fresh loaf.'

'A fresh loaf? No, we will not start a new loaf for just one slice. That will be all.'

'Yes, Sir.'

The housekeeper left him alone.

Ebenezer finished reading the papers and walked back to his residence, passing his security guards without a 'Good Night or a Merry Christmas.'

He walked through all the rooms of his private quarters, jiggling door handles, opening cupboards, even glancing under the tables and sofas. He did all this in near darkness as the deep gloom comforted him and it cost him nothing, which pleased him immensely. It was whilst he was checking under the large dining table he realised, with a start, just what he was doing, and shook his head in wonder. The image of Jacob floated across his mind's eye and he shivered.

'Time for bed,' he said aloud.

He entered his bedroom, a dark room containing little more than an antique four poster bed, a chest of drawers, a closet, outside which hung his dressing gown, a fireplace with a single flame flickering amongst the few pieces of wood and coal stacked within and his chair, tall-backed and overstuffed, showing signs of wear and several repairs.

Ebenezer settled into the armchair, lit only by the flickering embers of the pitiful fire and went to close his eyes when he noticed something strange on the TV.

The screen flickered then slowly an image took shape amidst swirling mist and fog, strangely mimicking the weather outside the building.

Ebenezer strained his eyes trying to make out the image before it came fully formed such was his lack of patience. He sat back in surprise when he recognised his old partner and previous occupant of the very residence he now lived. It was Jacob Marley.

"Ebenezeeeeeeeeeer."

Just the one word came from the image. One mournful word that filled the room and lingered, drawn out to such length he thought it might never end.

It had been seven years since Jacob had died and he had barely given him a moment's thought since the day of his death and here was his image for the second time that day. Marley's face was larger than life on the huge screen, his spectacles perched on his forehead, his wispy hair moved as if stirred by a breeze, but what captured Ebenezer were the eyes, wide open but motionless, their fixed stare looking right at him, through him it seemed. The image of the bust hauntingly appeared in Ebenezer's mind again, and he shivered.

The image did not speak again or move; it just looked at Ebenezer as if judging, weighing his thoughts as if about to pass judgement. Then he was gone. The screen was the same flat grey it had been when he first walked in.

Ebenezer pressed the "On" button for the TV, the "Play" button on the DVD but nothing happened, nothing changed.

'Bah!' he growled, and stood up and went through to his private bathroom to brush his teeth and change for bed, favouring the long nightgown his father and grandfather had worn as it still had plenty of wear in it. He even wore the cap with its conical point drooping down one side, to keep his head warm.

Walking back through his room, he frowned seeing his bedroom door was ajar. He pulled it open, looking into his sitting room when suddenly it whipped from his hand and slammed shut, the sound thunderous as it echoed around the huge residence, getting louder as it rolled along the corridors, and down the staircases, every room from basement to attic adding its own countenance, creating such a cacophony Ebenezer placed his hands over his ears trying to shut out the noise to no avail.

The sounds stopped abruptly, replaced by absolute silence.

Ebenezer paused before opening the door again and peered into the dark room. He gave himself a shake, not easily frightened and shut the door. Almost as an afterthought, he turned the key, locking it tight.

'Bah!' he said aloud.

'Humbug!' he said louder, and helped himself to a sweet.

Taking his seat again, he moved the chair closer to the small fire to feel its feeble heat on his legs. His housekeeper had laid out his milk; barely keeping its warmth from such a meagre flame. The fireplace was magnificent, but since taking office, Ebenezer had barely noticed the elaborate tiles that surrounded the grate, each hand painted, depicting scenes from the Bible, all he saw now was the image of his old friend Jacob Marley looking back from each and every tile.

His attention was drawn back to the screen as it flickered to life. A bell materialised, an old bell, like the big houses of old used to have to summon servants to a particular room. As it gained form it started to swing, just a little to start, scarcely making a sound and then more and more, the clapper inside banging the sides louder and louder until the room filled with its clanging. The echo of the first peel was joined by the second and then the third and fourth and fifth and more, until the room was filled with the peeling note of many such bells clambering together. The noise was so penetrating it was hard to think, and Ebenezer couldn't say whether it lasted a few seconds or a few minutes but before he had managed to grab the remote and turn off the volume. The bells ceased. The silence was so acute, so instant; Ebenezer felt unease within him.

Something I ate, he thought. *Cheese perhaps, or the meat turned, the milk soured.*

His attention was drawn back to the screen as he heard footsteps. Footsteps that started out with a hollow echo but as they came closer, each footfall rumbled like a distant storm, getting louder and louder as they came closer and closer, becoming claps of thunder that reverberated around the room.

Jacob was always one for the theatrics, Ebenezer thought, though despite his bravado, his unease grew.

He jumped as the logs on the small fire collapsed, sending tiny sparks shooting up the chimney.

The thunderous crash of each footfall stopped. The silence seemed more threatening than the noise before it.

On the screen was Jacob, as before, glasses atop his head, white wispy hair, gaunt sallow features looking towards the camera. Ebenezer had not realised just how ill Jacob had become; he looked so pale, grey almost, with no colour in his lips or cheeks to break up the dull pallor.

The eyes, once again, captured Ebenezer. Whilst they had never been warm and friendly eyes they had always held a fondness for him, but now they seemed just to stare. He felt a chill run down his spine. The eyes had the look of death foretold.

He became angry with himself; being afraid of his TV was ridiculous.

'Come on, Jacob out with it, what do you want with me?' he said aloud, pressing the mute button to return the sound.

As if in reply, the spectre of Jacob on the screen sat down and leaned forward, placing his elbows on his knees.

Ebenezer leaned in.

'Ebenezer, we were partners in life,' the image said, the voice barely more than a whisper yet it filled the room. The last word "life" stretched out as "lifeeeeeeeeeeeeeeeeeeeeeeeeeeeeeeeeeeee"

'We were,' said Ebenzer.

'We were so intent in our pursuits, so sure there was only one possible outcome to what we saw as the follies of the world, we closed our hearts and minds to everything else. Now that I am dead, I look back at the life I led, and my deeds weigh heavy on my soul, Ebenezer, very heavy indeed.'

Ebenezer shifted as if suddenly uncomfortable.

'I can only imagine the weight of the deeds you now have, after seven more years. I know you; I know you have not altered our course or changed our ways. Ebenezer, I have no words of comfort this night, I have no advice to give that would alter your course. It will come from other places Ebenezer, and from other sources. My time is short, even now I feel the pull of Death, and I cannot linger long.'

Ebenezer got up and walked around; as was his habit when he had to think, had to process information, make decisions.

'You're a bit slow in coming forward, Jacob, seven years, *seven years* and now you come forward and say something.'

Jacob left his chair.

'Ebenezer, you must listen. I have had no rest, no peace, nothing but the incessant torture of doubt and remorse. You must listen. I can make no amends for the life I have lived, the opportunities I misused; it is too late for me.'

Ebenezer looked at Jacob as he paced. 'Misused you say? Unemployment down, budget in its tenth year of surplus, inflation steady at half a percent, the Armed Forces bigger and better equipped than ever before, business is booming.'

Jacob continued as if he had not been interrupted, not heard the words his friend had just said. 'Business, Ebenezer, we focused on business when we should have been focused on humankind. Our policies were for the good of the country, not the world. They were about the money, when they should have been altruistic and philanthropic. Humanitarianism should have been our business, Ebenezer.'

Jacob coughed a racking, bone-rattling cough.

'I have little time, Ebenezer. It's not too late; I'm here to give you a second chance, one I hope you heed.'

Ebenezer stopped pacing; despite himself, he had to admit he was curious. He sat down opposite his old friend prepared to listen. Jacob had been a good friend.

'I have arranged for three Agents to visit.'

Ebenezer stood up and strode about again.

'They will visit one at a time,' Jacob continued.

'Bah, you should have arranged for them to come all at once, it would look less suspicious, a single meeting I can cover. *Three,* someone will notice.'

'They will come when the bell strikes one. One each night, for the next two nights and the last on the third night as the clock sounds the twelfth hour. You will see me no more, my dear friend; this is the last you will hear from me. Remember me.'

Ebenezer watched as Jacob backed away, then turned and walked down the long hallway. The sounds of metallic clanking filled the room drawing Ebenezer forward to look closer. He saw Jacob was dragging chains behind him, the links rasping as they uncoiled from huge piles, that rattled and clanked as he pulled them along. Ghostly images appeared; images of their youth, images of other people they had known together, people who had shared the same ideals as them but mostly, people who had suffered under their policies.

Ebenezer blinked, realising he was back in his own room, sitting in his own chair.

An effective use of old photos and film footage, there near transparent visage giving them impact, Ebenezer thought.

The screen faded to black, and all was silent.

'Bah,' said Ebenezer, getting up from the chair.

He jumped, startled, as the fire roared, the flames shooting up higher and higher casting the room into a red inferno of flickering flames, and deep within its heart, the image of Jacob, on his knees, weighed down and bound by thick heavy chains, his wails and cries filling the room as a fiery whip lashed his back.

'Believe, Ebenezer. Belieeeeeeeeeevvve.'

The fire winked out, a single tendril of smoke wound its way up the chimney.

CHAPTER FOUR

THE FIRST

Ebenezer was shocked into silence, shaken.

He went to the door, unlocked it, and looked out into the sitting room. Though it was dark and silent, Ebenezer paused for a moment, studying the darkness before closing the door and locking it tight. Everything was fine; he must have imagined the fire, his head cold affecting his mind.

That was it; he was sick.

Feeling the energy drain from him he went to bed. He pulled the heavy drapes of the four poster bed closed, something he seldom did, but this night he wanted their comfort, a comfort that harkened back to childhood when hiding under the blankets was all that was necessary to evade the scary shapes in the dark shadows.

Within moments of his head hitting the pillow, he was asleep.

*

When Ebenezer awoke, it was still dark. Disorientated, he pushed aside a curtain and looked around the room trying to distinguish the shapes of his furniture against the blackness of the night.

The clock on the mantle struck the hour, and he counted the chimes.

Twelve?

It was midnight?

He struggled to clear his mind; he had thought he retired later than midnight so how was it only twelve now?

Climbing out of bed, he navigated his way to the window, reaching out with his hands to feel for the chair and the dresser he knew to be there. Opening the curtains, he saw the dark of night outside. The glass had a coating of frost on the inside, and he had to wipe away a patch to see the thick fog had not abated since retiring. If anything, it seemed thicker. Surely, he had not slept the whole day through. Even Christmas day had its work schedule. Ebenezer was not one to take a day off, certainly not for something like Christmas and he had a full day planned, starting with breakfast at 6am sharp.

Ebenezer groped his way back to the warmth of his covers and pulled them over his frail body, ignoring the tendrils of cold that seemed to curl around him. He tried to think of a logical explanation and concluded he had simply gone to bed much earlier than he thought. At first, he dismissed the whole incident as a dream but his mind would not rest and replayed the evening over and over. Was it a dream or not?

Either way, Jacob had disturbed him more than he cared to admit.

Ebenezer tried to get back to sleep, but it eluded him as his mind continued to probe the passage of time and the message Jacob had given him.

*

The clock chimed the half hour, and he lay wide awake. He suddenly remembered Jacob's words. The first would visit him when the bell strikes one, half an hour from now. Determined to catch him coming into his room unannounced, he sat up and waited. Sleep had so far escaped him so he doubted he would have any trouble staying awake for thirty more minutes.

He listened to the seconds tick away, loud in the stillness of the night. He assumed he had dozed off and awoke as the full half hour had still yet to pass though it felt twice that time already. When the bell finally struck its single doleful note, it made him jump.

He gave a chuckle.

'For whom the bell tolls,' he said aloud.

'It tolls for thee, Ebenezer,' a voice finished.

Unseen hands pulled the curtains back and Ebenezer sat up, pulling the covers up to his chin as he searched the room, straining his eyes to pierce the darkness.

'Where are you? Show yourself.'

The scratch of a match being struck sounded out moments before there was a flare of light in the corner of the room, quickly diminishing to a small flame which seemed to float in the air for a second or two before the wick of a candle caught and cast it's glow. As the flame lengthened, spreading its light further into the corner, it picked out the figure that stood there.

Ebenezer looked at the man, for it was clearly a man. However, that was about the only thing that was clear.

The man looked both young and old. He was short, about 5ft 5', Ebenezer guessed. His hair was completely white and not regulation length as it hung down passed his neck and yet his face was unlined by the cares and woes most often seen on an older gentleman. Indeed his skin had the first flush of youth about it. Despite his short stature, he was well built, his huge arms and legs seemed to strain the material of his suit, and his belt buckle flashed and twinkled as it caught the candlelight, sending shafts of multi-coloured light into the room.

All in all, an odd looking fellow to be sure.

As the candle flickered, the agent seemed to fade into the darkness, one minute he only had one leg, the next only one arm, for one moment he seemed disembodied, just his head hovering in the air.

'Are you from the Agency? The spook Jacob warned me to expect?'

'I am, Sir.'

The voice was soft and gentle, barely above a whisper, so low it was as if it were coming from far away.

'Your name, spook?'

'I am Chris Ast, Sir.'

'And you have come to recap our policies, Chris?'

'No, Sir, *your* policies.'

Ebenezer grunted.

'Any in particular?'

'Your Welfare and Reclamation policies, Sir. Please rise and join me.'

Ebenezer considered refusing. It was the middle of the night; the bed was nice and warm, and the room was cold, and he was his nightgown, not something the public would ever see him in. But the voice, though gentle and soft, had steel to it that carried authority and command, even to a man as powerful as he.

He got out of bed, picked up his robe off the chair and slipped it on.

The spook pointed to the TV screen as it flickered to life.

'Sir, in 2005 we started Project Revelations where we predicted the world population would exceed 7 billion by 2012, a number reached by October

2011. By 2025, we are predicting it to exceed 8 billion. Your predecessor, Jacob Marley, implemented several policies to curb the growing population and accumulate vast wealth for the country at the same time. His welfare policies changed the nature of the benefits system, insisting all adults claiming benefits went to the workhouses and factories, even children were expected to work on weekends to qualify for Child Benefit and subsidies.'

The TV flickered and an image of child workers sitting in rows stitching trainers and T-shirts filled the screen. It changed to more workers, men, and women, doing laundry, loading sheets and pillowcases, hospital scrubs and more into huge machines. Changing again, teams of young teenagers were walking alongside the roads collecting rubbish and scrubbing graffiti off underpasses and walls.

'A crowning achievement. Those policies have saved the country millions by having benefit seekers do jobs our competitors were doing cheaper. Now we are cheaper. The industry benefits, the country benefits and the workers benefit, gaining self-respect and job experience,' Ebenezer said with pride.

The screen changed again. Male workers, men and boys, were crawling over huge piles of waste, which were so large the tops were lost within the confines of the screen. They were pulling out items that could be recycled or re-sold. Flies buzzed about their heads and rats scurried around their feet.

'Another success, using benefit seekers to sort through the rubbish the communities and industries were throwing away, netting millions in revenue.'

'These policies were groundbreaking in their scope and implementation. They were country wide within the second year,' intoned the spook without any passion or inflection and yet somehow damning.

'Every year, from 2006, there have been large scale outbreaks of plague amongst the reclamation workers. The death toll to date is over 10,000.'

'Not enough, not nearly enough,' Ebenezer grumbled under his breath.

The screen flickered and changed. A demonstration appeared on the screen, a demonstration against global warming. In the centre of the screen was a young woman.

'Not this, I don't need to be reminded of this.'

The screen continued to show the young woman chanting, surrounded by other demonstrators.

She was a small woman, in stark contrast to her brother, who had a stature more like President Lincoln of old. The other notable thing about the woman was that she was pregnant.

'Your sister, of frail health but a strong loving heart,' the Agent continued. 'She railed against all injustices including your Father's, with whom you didn't get along.'

Ebenezer grumbled something and folded his arms.

'He sent you to boarding school where you would have stayed had not little Fran intervened with your father to bring you home.'

'She did, I will not deny it. She was a wonderful child.'

'She died a woman, Ebenezer; just like your Mother, who died giving birth to you. Something your Father never forgave you for. She too had a child before she left this world,'

Ebenezer nodded.

'A boy, my nephew.'

'Indeed.'

'What has this to do with our plans, Mr Ast?'

The spook cast his arms wide.

'I am just following my instruction, Sir, to recount certain events that have led you to this point.'

'Instructions? Instructions from whom?'

'Prime Minister Marley, Mr Prime Minister.'

'Prime Minister Marley has been dead these past seven years, how is he giving orders from beyond the grave?'

'Their origin is indisputable.'

Ebenezer waved his hand impatiently.

The screen changed again.

Ebenezer leaned forward, a rare smile crossing his face.

'Do you recognise the place, Mr Prime Minister?'

'Yes of course,' Ebenezer replied, leaning closer, his focus fixed upon the images on the screen.

CHAPTER FIVE

MAYOR FEZZIWIG

'I was born here,' said Ebenezer, gazing at the scene before him. A cold crisp bright winter's day, snow glistening on the ground, shaggy ponies trotting along with boys upon their backs, laughing and calling out to others riding in carts and those walking alongside.

To Ebenezer it was as if he was there all over again, he could feel the snow crunch beneath his feet; see his breath mist before his eyes.

The jubilant shouts of the boys drew him forward, and he found himself amongst them, the air filled with merry music and laughter. Ebenezer called out to those he recognised, waving to gain their attention.

'They cannot see you, Mr Prime Minister.'

Ebenezer heard the voice but paid it no heed. He called out Merry Christmas in response to many such calls passed from one to another, his heart leaping and bounding with life and vitality, his vision blurred, causing him to wipe his eyes, only for them to blur again within moments.

The scene changed to one of a school, empty but for the presence of a lone boy, neglected by all.

Emotions flooded Ebenezer, emotions he had not felt for many a year and his eyes filled again.

'Brother? Brother dear? I have come to fetch you.'

Ebenezer watched the boy stand as the young girl threw her arms around his neck and kissed him on the cheek.

'I've come to bring you home, dear Brother, Father sent me.'

'Home, Fran, really?'

'Yes, Home, won't that be lovely? Father is so changed, Ebby you will hardly recognise him. He sent me to bring you home, the car is outside waiting. Come, Ebby, hurry and get your things.'

The scene changed again.

'A strange place,' said the Agent, 'for a Mayor and his aides to be? Do you know it?'

'Know it, of course I know it.'

He entered the building and saw an old gentleman in a white wig, dressed in a red suit, standing behind a long table.

'Mr Fezziwig,' Ebenezer cried out with pleasure.

They watched as Mr Fezziwig ladled out thick brown soup teeming with vegetables and lumps of meat to the men and women who lined up, bowls in hand.

'Eb, Dick, put down those phones. No more work tonight. It's Christmas Eve, young Dick. Does Christmas not mean anything to you, young Eb? Come help set up more tables; we need plenty.'

Ebenezer watched his younger self and, his friend and fellow aide; Dick, rush over to pull tabletops from the pile, snapping out their legs, and standing them in rows. One, two three; were standing free, lickety-split four, five and six were standing proud, seven, eight and nine, all in a line. The two boys went rushing over to the Mayor breathing hard, to stand either side and hand out fresh crusty bread and mugs of hot tea to every one of the poor homeless souls. Merry music played in the background, and as the food and drink were consumed, the sound of voices rose as everyone joined in with the songs; carols and modern tunes alike.

'Ebenezer?'

'What? Oh, nothing. There were carol singers in the lobby earlier. I chased them out. Wish I hadn't, that's all.'

The Agent regarded him silently, inclining his head in a shallow nod before returning his gaze to the scene unfolding before him.

Some of the men and women moved aside tables and danced, whilst others clapped along. Even Mayor Fezziwig had a turn and was cheered and clapped by all as he shimmied and shook across the dance floor.

Everyone was having so much fun and the whole time Ebenezer was as much part of the festivities as young Eb was. He remembered it all like it was yesterday. He could feel the joy in the room; hear the music playing and enjoyed it as much as he had all those years past.

Indeed, it was only when Dick and Eb slipped through the crowds and into the kitchens to help with the washing up that Ebenezer became conscious of the Agent watching him.

'Such a small act hardly warrants such an outpouring of thanks and gratitude,' said the Agent.

'Small?' said Ebenezer.

'Sure, this cost the Mayor nothing in relative terms, he was such a wealthy man. Even though he paid for the shelter, food and drink out of his own pocket, is that really deserving of such praise and recognition?'

'It's not about the money,' said Ebenezer exasperated. 'The Mayor had the power and position to make us happy or miserable, our time with him productive or burdensome, a day of accomplishment or one of toil, satisfaction ord dissatisfaction. He extended his influence to others outside his circle of privilege and power. His greatness was not in his wealth as generous as he was, but his way with words and action, often so small and insignificant they went unnoticed but would result in such positive results people often wondered how they had come to pass. Those outcomes would have been worth it at twice the cost, thrice even.'

Ebenezer looked into the distance, his thoughts occupied.

'What's on your mind?' asked the Agent.

'Nothing really.'

'Must be something to trouble you so?'

'I was thinking of my driver, that's all.'

The Agent looked at Ebenezer.

'My time is almost at an end. We should move on.'

Ebenezer found himself looking at a young man sitting next to a pretty girl dressed in black.

'You value your career more than you do me,' she said softly.

'Not true, Belle, though I endeavour to better myself, my standing, to rise within the political circles. And yes, to earn more money to safeguard myself against the uncertainties of life.'

'You fear life too much,' she replied. 'You have lost your ideals, shortened your view of the world to that of your own self. You no longer support the people and endeavours of your principles. Now you throw your support to any that gains you the most political advantage. When did you last make time for family, for friends, for me?'

'That just makes me wise,' Ebenezer replied angrily. 'It does not mean I love you less.'

'You don't see it, but you love me less and your career more. It's as clear as day When we were younger we talked of working together now you forge ahead alone.'

'We were kids then.'

'And now we are grown up and have grown apart.'

'Have I ever said I wanted to end our relationship?' he asked.

'In words no,' she replied. 'But in your actions, your nature, your outlook on life, all scream you wish to be free. If we met today you would not look at me the same way as when we first met, would not pursue me as you did back then.'

'You think not?'

'I want to think otherwise, Eb, but were you free today, yesterday, tomorrow, it's impossible to think you would choose a girl without political connection.'

The girl's voice broke, and she looked away.

The Agent and Ebenezer could see the tears in her eyes and upon her cheeks.

'I hope you are happy with the life you have chosen, Eb, I truly do.'

She got up and walked away.

Ebenezer turned to the Agent.

'Why do you show me these things? What relevance do they have with my Welfare and Reclamation policies?'

As if he didn't hear, the Agent said, 'I have one more.'

'No more. I am tired and wish to return to my bed. I will watch no more.'

Another scene unfolded before his eyes, and he watched as a Mother and daughter sat watching the playfulness of other children as they ran around the large living room, excited at the prospect of Santa Claus's visit that very evening.

Ebenezer, at first mistook the young girl as that of his old girlfriend, but looking closer, he saw it was the Mother, Belle, older now, whom he had once loved. She had grown even lovelier to his eyes with the passage of time.

The door opened, and a man entered, tall and handsome, carrying bags and parcels. Screaming their welcome, the children mobbed him in their eagerness to divest him of all he carried, so they could throw their arms around him, hugging him dearly.

Shooing away the younger children, the mother, and eldest daughter rescued the man and guided him to an armchair by the fire.

Ebenezer felt the tendrils of jealousy as he watched, longing to be that husband and father. To have a family who so clearly loved him.

He couldn't watch any longer.

'Turn it off, Agent,' he commanded.

'It will not change anything, Sir. These are images of things past. Of your making, not mine.'

'It's too hard to watch, turn it off now!'

The Agent watched Ebenezer, unmoved and unmoving.

Ebenezer blinked, realising he was in his bedroom, sitting in front of the TV, the scene still in the room, with the family laughing and enjoying their Christmas Eve.

With an anguished cry, he jumped up, grabbed the blanket off his bed, and threw it over the screen.

Although the image was gone, he could still see the light of the screen escaping from under the blanket.

Tiredness overcame him, and he staggered to bed, falling asleep before he could remove his dressing gown.

CHAPTER SIX

THE SECOND VISIT

Ebenezer awoke abruptly and sat up, wide awake and alert.

The memory of his earlier visit was vivid in his mind as was the expectation of another. He saw by the clock it was not yet one and planned to challenge the next Agent as he appeared in his room. Their apparent freedom to come and go within his house unseen was truly vexing.

He pulled aside the curtains that enveloped his bed and returned to the warmth of his covers, his eyes scanning the bedroom, waiting for the next visit.

He was prepared for all manner of entry; from secret panels to moving fire surrounds but when the clock struck one Ebenezer felt the first flutter of nerves. Five minutes passed then ten without any sign of the Agent.

Ebenezer lay bathed in the ruddy glow of the fire, scanning the room, the minutes ticking by, fifteen then twenty, thirty then forty, until a full hour had passed.

As he lay there, his mind began to think, to wonder, and he looked more closely at the fire, which, from his vantage, seemed to be all but extinguished.

So where was the red light coming from?

He got out of bed and saw the red light was coming from a crack along the floor. As he approached, he noticed, even fainter, the red lines travelled up both sides and across the top, framing a doorway within the wood panelling.

'I knew it,' he said aloud, 'a secret passageway.'

As he pushed and probed the panelling, it opened and in slipped a huge man. It wasn't that he was just large, he was tall as well, framed by the red glow behind him, he looked like someone stepping out of the very fires of hell.

So when the Agent laughed heartedly and said cheerily, 'Hello, Ebenezer, come, come, shake my hand and welcome,' he could not have been any more surprised.

Bewildered, Ebenezer shook his hand, taking in the girth of the man, the green of his suit, the torch in his hand, curiously shaped like a horn, and his hat, with a twig of holly stuck into the band. But it was his eyes that captivated him, so kind and gentle, they humbled Ebenezer, and he had to look away.

'I am MI5 Agent Chris Resent,' the man said, his voice a deep rumble that seemed filled with humour. 'I'm guessing you've never seen an Agent quite like me before?'

Ebenezer shook his head. 'No, Sir, I must say I have not.'

'Not surprising, there are many agents, Ebenezer, brothers, and sisters all.'

'Quite the family.'

'Indeed.'

'Agent,' said Ebenezer softly, 'deliver your message if you will. Last night I was not so compliant, and I learnt my lesson. Tonight I am ready to listen, to listen, and learn.'

'Come then, let's get started.'

Ebenezer took his seat before the roaring blaze of the fire. Before his mind could ponder on the origin of such a blaze or indeed the food that sat on the table by his side, his attention was drawn to the TV screen.

Ebenezer blinked as the image on the screen showed the city streets.

The image was small at first, and Ebenezer leaned forward.

Down smaller streets, the fog still lingered but in the main thoroughfares, only the odd wisp of mist remained.

Captivated by the sights, he could almost imagine he could feel the crunch of the snow beneath his feet, the chill in the air. Indeed, he ducked as a snowball went flying past.

The Agent laughed heartedly. 'They cannot see you, Ebenezer.'

Ebenezer chuckled at his own foolishness and watched as the young boys and girls screamed with joy and delight as they dashed here and there, gathering snow from the piles heaped on the side of the roads, and throwing them at each other, the jubilant cry of success as one found its mark mixing with the laughter.

Every corner had a fire, lit within a brazier, which crackled and popped merrily, casting their orange glow over the men seeking their warmth, and the sounds of carols being sung could be heard floating in the air.

The music of the streets, thought Ebenezer and was instantly surprised at himself for such poetic nonsense.

The supermarket was closed for the evening, shutters were drawn, lights winking out one by one and, as if called by the church bell peeling in the distance calling its worshippers to mass, folk emerged from the side streets and alleyways.

They jostled and shoved a little but in truth they had little energy to waste on anger or violence, they were just eager to get to the bins where the supermarket had thrown out all the food that was near or passed its expiration date.

And the selection was a feast for the eyes.

Bread of many shapes, cakes of all sizes, tins aplenty; contents often unknown as the labels were missing lay beside packs of biscuits, mostly broken and smashed to crumbs. Vegetables of every type, most showing hardly any kind of spoil at all. Packs and packages of all manner of foodstuff, that were split or torn, provided a bounty for the poor. Even the tea crates were upturned, the loose tea in the bottom carefully collected in cups and pots.

The spoiled meat was left for the rats by the poor folk as they often made the eater sick and to fatten up the rats, which were a staple in their daily diet.

Such was the quantity that evening everyone was able to take home some fare to feed their families and celebrate Christmas in some small way.

'Such waste,' said Ebenezer.

'The food or the people?' the Agent asked.

Ebenezer felt something wash through him, a feeling he was not accustomed to and chose to remain silent.

'The supermarket manager throws out extra every year,' said the Agent, 'knowing the poor wretches need this bounty to survive over the Christmas period.'

The scene changed again, and Ebenezer stood in the living room of his own chauffeur and aide, for Bob had both duties to uphold.

He saw Bob's wife, Mrs Cratchit, dressed in her best clothing, though Ebenezer could see the elbows were a little threadbare and her skirt frayed along the hem, laying a cloth over the table with the help of a younger girl he assumed was Bob's daughter. One of them at least, he was dimly aware Bob had children but how many or their names were lost to him.

'That's Belinda,' said the Agent. 'Mr Cratchit's second eldest daughter.'

Ebenezer nodded and watched as a young man came into the room holding a saucepan.

'What do you think, are these potatoes boiled enough?'

He handed his Mum a knife who stuck it into the pan.

'Yes, they're soft enough, now into the oven with them, and we'll have some lovely roast potatoes to go with the chicken.'

'That's Peter,' said the Agent.

Ebenezer looked at the boy, noticing the trousers he was wearing were far too big for him, as was the jacket, and guessed they were hand-me-downs from his father.

Two smaller kids came rushing in, tearing around the table in their excitement. One boy, one girl, both dressed similarly with clothes long since passed down by their two older sisters.

'The chicken smells lovely,' cried the boy.

'I want the skin,' cried the girl.

'A leg for me,' cried Peter, laughing.

Mrs Cratchit hugged Belinda and said aloud, 'I wonder what's keeping your father.'

The door opened at that very moment, and Ebenezer expected to see Bob walking through, but it was another young woman.

'Martha, Martha you're home,' cried the youngest boy, throwing his arms around her waist.

'Martha!' screamed the youngest girl, circling around behind her, and throwing her arms around her.

Laughing delightedly, Martha hugged her young brother and sister before unpeeling their arms from around her so she could go to her mother.

'Why so late?' said Mrs Cratchit, hugging her eldest to her and kissing her cheek.

'Trains again,' said Martha. 'You would think on a night such as this, every guard and every driver would show up for work.'

'Well, you're home now,' said Mrs Cratchit.

'Dad's here, Dad's here,' cried the two youngsters and Ebenezer could not stop the smile that creased his face at their pleasure of his return.

Bob Cratchit walked into the living room with a young boy on his shoulders.

'Another son!' Ebenezer was shocked. On what he paid him he was surprised he could afford any children let alone this brood.

'That's Tim,' said the Agent.

Ebenezer looked up sharply. 'Why is there sadness in your voice?'

The Agent ignored him.

Ebenezer drew in a breath to berate the Agent. Not used to being ignored, he was not about to be now, but the conversation in the room caught his attention.

'How was Tim at church?' asked Mrs Cratchit.

'As good as gold,' said Bob. 'You know I think he is growing stronger by the day. He said an odd thing on the way home though. He said he hoped those at the church would look upon him and remember who it was who healed the sick on this day of days.'

Ebenezer looked at the Agent again.

'Why does his voice tremble so?'

Again, the Agent ignored him.

Tim sat closest to the fire so it might warm him, a blanket tucked around him by the young boy and girl before they dashed off after Peter, yelling for him to wait.

Ebenezer watched Bob closely and could see him master himself, gather his thoughts, and then smile, though his eyes glistened.

'Well, family, come, come let us eat our fill and be merry this night.'

Right on cue, Peter walked into the room baring a whole chicken upon a plate; the younger boy behind carried a bowl of roast potatoes steaming away, the young girl a bowl of peas, green and vibrant.

Everyone helped. Eager hands took the bowls from the youngsters and placed them on the table. Peter, allowed the honour of placing the chicken at the head of the table, did so, ready for Bob to carve. Mrs Cratchit nipped out for the gravy, thick and brown as good gravy should be and Bob helped Tim to his seat before taking his at the head of the table.

He took a moment to look around at his family, pride, and pleasure shining clearly from his face before starting to carve.

As the knife sliced through the succulent breast of the chicken, a murmur of delight arose around the table.

Even Tim managed a cry of pleasure and together with the two younger siblings started to chant 'Chicken, chicken, chicken.'

'One would think they had never had chicken before,' said Ebenezer joyfully, enjoying the merriment and happiness around the table.

'Oh, they have had chicken before. Bob saves up to buy one at Christmas and Easter. Sometimes there is small bird unsold at the butchers that he buys at other times, but it's a treat every time they have it.'

Ebenezer mulled over this news. Chicken was plentiful and cheap, yet his own aide and driver couldn't afford it as a common staple.

Bob sliced the chicken making sure everyone got a slice of breast or a leg. The wings and all the bones saved to flavour the broth, Mrs Cratchit would make for dinner the next day and the day after that. Martha handed around the potatoes, encouraging the younger ones to take their fill, whilst Peter spooned peas onto every one's plate, as they were plentiful.

Ebenezer could see a cloud pass over Bob's face as he surveyed the half-filled plates before his children and his wife, who, nevertheless, gazed upon their fare as if it were a feast.

Bob's own plate was barely a quarter full and if he could, he would have gone without completely, to give his family just a little more, but he knew such a gesture would only upset them, highlight their poverty and lower the festive spirit. With a brave smile, he laughed as Tim told of his ride home upon his shoulders, and the snowballs the other kids had thrown at them in play, as everyone tucked in.

Once the first pangs of hunger were satisfied Bob raised his glass. 'A toast!' he cried.

'A toast,' his family echoed, all reaching for their cups, mugs and glasses as such was the combination they had.

'A Merry Christmas to us all.'

'Merry Christmas,' the family cried.

And Tim finished with,

'And God Bless us every one.'

Bob stroked the top of his baldhead and then kissed it, and again Ebenezer could see the unshed tears in Bob's eyes.

'Spook, what's wrong with Tim? Why is he so thin? So tiny?' Ebenezer asked gruffly, his voice gravelly.

'Cancer.'

'But we have the cure for cancer.'

'Indeed, but your welfare policies prohibit the drugs necessary to only those that can afford private purchase.'

'But he will live though?'

'Unlikely. Without the proper treatment, there will be an empty place at the Cratchit table.'

'No don't say that. There must be hope, say there's hope.'

'Unless policies change he will die and decrease the surface population of the planet.'

Ebenezer had been about to interrupt, but hearing his own words thrown back at him stopped him cold, and he stared at the Agent open mouthed before looking away, tears of his own pricking his eyes.

'You see before you the results of *your* policies, the consequences of *your* reforms. People are not numbers to be assessed and gauged. Who are you to determine who is worthy to live and who should die? Who deserves to stay on this ball of rock and who should leave to make way? Is the naked child sitting in the mud and waste, playing with a couple of twigs, any less innocent and deserving of life to one dressed and playing with his game console? It may be, Ebenezer that you are less deserving of life than those who have suffered and died under your Welfare and Reform Policies.'

Ebenezer looked at the Cratchits, the happiness of the children though they had nothing much to be happy about to his eyes. The pride within Mrs Cratchit's face not only for her children but also for her husband, Bob, though he provided such a meagre living for them. The pride within Bob, for his children and his wife, who, despite having so little, loved each other so fiercely, played together so well, that their house was as happy and filled with laughter as any of the richer folk, more so perhaps, as they depended on each other to make their lives' rich and rewarding.

'Another toast,' cried Peter, holding aloft his cup without a handle.

Bob raised his glass and thought for a moment.

'To Mr Scrooge,' he said, 'for without his benevolence we would not have this feast before us.'

There was silence around the table.

The thud of Peter's cup as he set it back on the table sounded like a Judge's gavel.

'Mr Scrooge is the worst thing that has happened to this country,' said Mrs Cratchit. 'His policies have starved his people; thousands have died. And for what? So he can sit on a pile of gold coin? What is the point of having such a surplus if it's not used? Not only for the betterment of the country but for the world?'

'No politics at the table,' admonished Bob gently. 'Besides, it's Christmas Day,' he added with a cheer that sounded forced even to Ebenezer.

'Christmas day? Surely the only day in the whole year one might; *might* I say, wish good health on such a greedy, selfish, hard-hearted, miserable excuse for a man.'

Ebenezer could see Bob looking at her steadily until she relented.

'Fine then. To Mr Scrooge, a Merry Christmas, and a Happy New Year. There, happy now? I am sure he is very happy and very merry counting his coin someplace.'

The children were silent, watching both their parents like it was a tennis match, looking left as their Dad spoke, and then right as their Mum responded.

Martha broke the spell, picking up her mug.

'To Mr Scrooge,' she said, and took a sip.

Each of the children followed suit though there was none of the happiness and joy that had preceded that moment.

'I have not met Mr Scrooge,' said Tim. 'But I don't think I like him if he brings such unhappiness to you, Mum.'

'Come,' said Mrs Cratchit. 'I refuse to let that man spoil our Christmas. Who's for pudding?'

The very words transformed the atmosphere, and everyone cheered and banged their spoons on the table, even Bob joined in as Mrs Cratchit smiled in delight at such a response and rose to collect plates and fetch the pudding.

Peter, Martha, and Bel rose to help and soon the dinner things were cleared away and the Christmas pudding was grandly presented, blue flames flickering about its crown.

The three youngest clapped their hands in joy and pleasure upon seeing the pudding alight. Bob rose and moved around the table to hug and kiss his wife.

'What a wonderful pudding dear, you're a marvel.'

'I was so worried it would not rise, or it would burn,' she confessed. 'I get to make pudding so rarely.'

'It's perfect,' Bob said.

Everyone agreed calling out his or her thanks to Mum for making such a pudding.

'It smells heavenly,' cried Tim, taking a big sniff.

'It looks so lovely,' said the youngest girl, holding her hands over her mouth to stop herself from dribbling, such was her mouth watering at the sight and smell of such a treat.

Bob sliced into the pudding, cutting it evenly for the kids, even managing a thin piece for Mrs Cratchit and an even thinner piece for himself.

'No no, you must have more,' cried Martha, cutting a section of hers and placing it on her Mum's plate.

'Yes, without you both we would not have such a feast,' said Peter, cutting a generous potion off his own slice and pushing it onto Bob's plate.

'Oh, but now you have less, Peter,' said Bel, cutting off a piece of hers and reaching across the table placed it in his bowl.

Bob and Mrs Cratchit laughed and called a halt to the pudding swapping.

'Ok, ok, I think we all have a very generous slice now, thank you all so very much. I am very proud of you, and if I don't tell you that enough, and how much I love you all, then know it in your hearts that it is true.'

'Daaaaad, you say it... like all the time,' said Peter, shaking his head ruefully.

Bel laughed. 'It's true, so, embarrassing. In front of my friends as well, all the time.'

Bob laughed. 'Good then, I can go to my grave knowing you know how much I love you all.'

'Bob!' scolded Mrs Cratchit. 'Don't talk like that. Grave indeed.'

Bob laughed again, and the mood was as festive as it had ever been. More so, in fact, as they tucked into their pudding, all smacking their lips after their three spoonfuls had cleared their plates or bowls.

'Lovely,' said Bel.

'Delicious,' said Peter.

Martha laughed and thought, 'Splendid,' she said.

Bob joined in the game. 'Marvellous,' he said.

'Great,' said the youngest boy.

'Ummmm, scrumptious,' said the youngest girl and everyone clapped and said what a great word that was.

Everyone looked at Tim expectantly.

Ebenezer thought furiously for a word himself, one that had not already been said.

'I cannot think of one,' Ebenezer admitted, then yelled, 'Delightful, Delightful,' and laughed aloud, though no one around the table heard him of course.

'Splendicious,' said Tim laughing. 'It was truly splendicious.'

'Ooo, you cannot make up words,' said Peter

'Nooo, it has to be a real word,' said Martha laughing.

'No, no made-up words,' said Ebenezer, laughing. 'Though it is a good one, splendicious indeed.'

'It is a real word. I read it in the book. Quentin James and the Jacobite Gold, so it has to be a real word,' argued Tim. 'So that's my word; Splendicious.'

'Well, I like it,' said Bob. 'I think the whole meal was splendicious. Thank you, my dear, for such a wonderful meal.'

'Here here,' said Peter, raising his cup.

'To Mum for such a wonderful meal,'

'To Mum,' cried everyone in unison.

Martha reached over to stroke Mum's back as she dabbed her eyes.

'I nearly forgot, I heard there is an opening at the Refuse Reclamation Yard, Peter.'

'Oh no, not there,' said Mrs Cratchit.

Bob held his hands up.

'It's in the office; they are looking for a junior clerk to help out.'

Mrs Cratchit looked none too pleased.

'We will talk about it later,' she said with finality.

Martha teased Peter with tales of long hours and work of such mundane and drudgery he would struggle to stay awake, though she was smiling whilst she said it.

They continued to sit at the table telling each other about their day, their schoolwork. They teased Bel about her boyfriend and Peter about making doe eyes at a girl he liked down the street. It was a heart-warming sight, a family sitting together, sharing their thoughts and feelings, and laughing good naturedly together. Not a thought was given to the toes poking out of Bob's socks, neither the worn elbows of their jumpers and cardigans, nor the wearing of woolly hats and gloves whilst still inside, as the evening got colder. They were a family, grateful to have one another and happy to be together.

CHAPTER SEVEN

THE CHRISTMAS SPIRIT

Even though the snow fell, the air was crisp, and darkness had descended, the streets were not empty but filled with people knocking on friends and neighbours doors and cries of Merry Christmas rang out from more sources than Ebenezer could see.

Children ran in the snow, making snowman and throwing snowballs, whilst the Mums and Dads gathered in huddles, sharing their warmth as they swapped tales of their Christmas meals and enjoyed each other's company.

*

Ebenezer blinked as the scene changed, reminding him that he was sitting in his room, and not standing in the middle of the street.

The screen flickered from image to image, all of families, many as poor as, or poorer than the Cratchits, celebrating Christmas. Each one was a scene of merriment and good cheer. Last of the scenes was of a family he knew, his nephew's.

Recognising his nephew, Ebenezer leaned forward.

His nephew was laughing heartedly and so infectious was his laugher all those around him chuckled and laughed and even Ebenezer himself felt his mouth crease into a smile and the bubbles of laughter stir in his chest.

'Honestly, I kid you not. He Bah's like a grumpy sheep even at the mention of Christmas. BAH! He says.'

'I'm not surprised, Fred,' his wife called across the room. 'Miserable old bugger.'

Ebenezer frowned. 'Do all wives have tongues so sharp?' he asked to no one in particular. 'Pretty though, I grant you. I can see what Fred see's in her.'

'She has more than just looks,' said the Agent, causing Ebenezer to hang his head slightly as he heard the tone of rebuke within his voice.

'Of course, of course. No Nephew of mine would marry just for looks. She has a brain in her head; anyone can see that. I was just saying is all.'

The Agent gave Ebenezer a withering look before turning back to the scene before them.

'He is an odd fellow,' conceded Fred. 'I cannot deny that. But for all his faults...'

'Of which there are many,' cried one of the guests.

'Of which there are many,' echoed Fred. 'Thank you, Graham. He has made his own bed and lies within it. But he is family, so here, in my home at least, I will not say a word against him and would ask you all to respect that.'

'He, and Marley before him, took us out of recession and debt,' said his wife, 'and made the country very rich.'

'To what end?' asked Fred, his voice rising in exasperation despite his own request moments earlier. 'What good is having all that money if it's not used to make everyone at least comfortable,' he said, 'given out to benefit those in need?'

'Well, I think he started off with good intentions,' said Graham thoughtfully. 'Him and Marley. The Benefit system was rife with freeloaders and layabouts. Immigrants were flocking to the country, not to work but to cash in on our welfare. Monies, supposed to help the young and old in this country, were being sent back to their home countries, our taxes sustaining other country's welfare needs, as well as groaning under the weight of our own.'

'True, reforms were needed and once they were in place the relief to the system was noticeable, but then it went too far,' said Beth. 'Once we were out of recession, once the deficit was paid off, we needed to rethink. Not revert back to the old ways but come up with new ways to improve the wellbeing of everyone, raising the standard of living for the poorer amongst us, whilst creating jobs and ensuring people worked, and having children was something considered and planned.'

'Oh, you are wading into dangerous territory there, Beth,' said Fred, laughing.

'Well, I have no patience for the man and come the elections I will be glad to see the back of him, said another guest.'

'Well I feel sorry for him,' said Fred. 'True, I may not agree with his policies; and his mean spirit and miserable demeanour only hurts himself, shunning friends and family alike. I invited him for dinner you know?'

'Oh, Fred, you didn't did you? What if he turns up? He will spoil Christmas for everyone,' said Fred's wife looking at the door.

'You know Uncle, he will never come, he never does, and that's my point. Who does he hurt other than himself by refusing? I am sure we are better company than the loneliness of his house. You know he sacked nearly all the staff there. It is just him, the housekeeper, two security guards and Chauffeur and aide Bob Cratchit.'

'We know; he made a speech about looking after one's self, when he dismissed them, with not a thought for their livelihood and families that depended upon their jobs.'

'He kept poor old Bob Cratchit, though he has to do the job of two people and take a pay cut to boot,' said Fred, a thread of heat entering his voice. 'But I will invite him every year nevertheless; that's a promise.'

'Come,' said Fred's wife. 'Let's put on some music and dispel such thoughts of Uncle Scrooge.'

Music filled the air, and a couple of the girls got up and danced. Before long, they had others up and joining in.

As Ebenezer watched and listened to the music, he thought upon all he had been shown by the two Agents. Odd thoughts teased his mind. Thoughts suggesting other options, other policies that could have achieved the same ends without the level of harshness and isolation his had brought. Perhaps he too could have been happy.

Then Bob suggested playing some Christmas games.

Blind man's bluff had them all teasing Thomas as he unerringly sought out Fred's sister-in-law Plum. They all knew he was sweet on her.

Ebenezer laughed along with the group as she dodged here and there, causing Thomas to bang into all manner of furniture before allowing herself to be caught within his arms and returning his kiss with ardour.

'Why do they call her Plum?' asked Ebenezer.

'She so loved the fruit as a baby it was one of the first words she spoke and it stuck as a nickname ever since,' said the Agent.

Ebenezer smiled, hearing the distant memory of being called Eb by his friends or Ebby, as his sister preferred.

Other games were played, and everyone joined in with much merriment, including Ebenezer, who yelled out answers and guesses along with everyone else with equal vigour and passion.

The scene started to dim.

'Oh can't we watch some more? Please, Agent Resent, look they are starting a new game.'

Such was Ebenezer's enthusiasm the Agent could not deny him and allowed the scene to continue.

Ebenezer leaned forward; his forehead creased in concentration as Fred called out the rules.

'The game is simple. You have to guess what I am by asking me questions,' Fred said, 'though I can only answer yes or no.'

'Sounds simple enough,' said Ebenezer, edging forward a little more in his seat.

'Are you a woman,' asked Thomas.

'No.'

'Are you alive?' asked his wife

'Yes.'

More questions were fired at him from all sides, some more loudly than others and none more so than Ebenezer himself.

'Beast, ask if he is a beast,' he called out loudly.

'Are you a beast?' asked Plum.

'Yes.'

'Finally!' said Ebenezer, quite exhausted. 'See I was right,' he said to the Agent, who smiled at his exuberance.

'What could it be?' said Ebenezer, looking at Plum, as more questions ascertained it was an beast that growled, that prowled the streets of London, it had never been sold for meat or kept as a pet.

'What kind of beast is so mean and grumpy, prowling the streets of London, grunting most often and likes sweets?'

He looked at the Agent, who was looking at him.

'It's me!' cried Ebenezer, jumping up and down, 'IT'S ME!' he said louder, trying to make them hear.

Fred was laughing heartedly as they asked more questions and guessed many animals, all wrong.

'Plum, Plum, it's me, say it's me, quick before the five minutes are up.'

Whether she heard a distant voice or by coincidence, Plum suddenly jumped up crying out, 'I know, I know, it's your Uncle. It's Uncle Ebenezer!'

'Yes!' said Fred jubilantly. 'Well done Plum.'

Everyone laughed and clapped.

'That was a good one, Fred.'

'Well thought of, Fred.'

'An excellent game.'

'A toast to my Uncle, who has provided us with such fun though he has denied us the pleasure of his company. Ebenezer Scrooge, a Merry Christmas, and a Happy New Year.'

'Hear Hear.'

'To Mr Scrooge.'

'Mr Scrooge.'

'Merry Christmas, Fred,' Ebenezer called out. 'Merry Christmas to you all,' he added, laughing and wiping a tear from his eye.

The screen went black, and Ebenezer blinked in surprise to find himself back in his cold dark room and not in the warm, pleasant room of his nephews. He didn't stop to wonder at the fire that had all but died out or the food that had all but disappeared.

'My time grows short,' said the Agent. 'I have one last thing to show you.'

The screen started to grow brighter, and Ebenezer leaned in.

CHAPTER EIGHT

IGNORANCE AND WANT

Ebenezer found himself in the midst of a camp.

'Where are we, Agent?' Ebenezer asked.

The Agent ignored him.

Ebenezer looked around at the tents, many ripped and patched, other dwellings little more than boxes, and everywhere, there were men, most sitting in the dust and dirt. A few kids were kicking a can about between them. A mountain dominated the skyline.

The odd thing was the silence, only broken by the pitiful cries of a child and hacking coughing that Ebenezer could not pinpoint as it came from so many sources.

'Which country is this?' he asked. 'Where are the aid workers?'

'Country? Why, this is your country, Ebenezer. This is one of your Reclamation camps.'

Ebenezer looked about him again, seeing it more clearly. The mountain was a huge pile of rubbish, the pot sitting on the fire; a cast away, dented and missing its handle, everything from the tents, just old sheets or the lucky find of an old tarpaulin, to the beds within, boxes mostly, the odd mildew mattress here and there, all cast offs.

Every person he saw was thin, dirty and covered in scratches and sores, but it was the eyes that tore at him most. The lost look, the hopelessness they conveyed, the abject misery they held that pulled at his heart.

'This is the result of the Welfare and Reform Policies?' said Ebenezer aghast.

'This is the result of YOUR policies, Ebenezer.'

Ebenezer hung his head knowing it to be true. He wanted to say he never knew it was this bad, that if he had known he would have changed things but even in his own head, he knew that was not true. The truth was he hadn't wanted to know and deliberately kept himself ignorant of the repercussions of his policies.

'Have they no other choices, no other opportunities?' Ebenezer asked.

'Are there no workhouses, no factories, no debtors prisons,' said the Agent, biting off each word, for the first time losing control of his emotions.

Ebenezer jumped as the clock sounded out its doleful DONG! Looking at the time he saw it was twelve o'clock.

'Agent,' Ebenezer said, and stopped in surprised realising he was alone in his room. The Agent had left.

'Twelve O'clock. Jacob said the last Agent would come at twelve.'

He searched the room, seeing no one at first, but then on a closer look, in the corner, in the darkest corner he saw movement. Black within the blackness stirred, to form a shape, to become a person and Ebenezer found himself staring at a man, for man he must be. Old, older than the other agents by far. His face was white, except around the eyes, which were dark as if sleep had long since been denied him, and his skin looked so thin, drawn so tight, Ebenezer feared it would split before his eyes.

The Agent left the darkness as if he was entering the room from another place.

CHAPTER NINE

THE LAST AGENT

The Agent moved past Ebenezer without speaking to stand by the TV, turning to regard him silently.

'And your name, Agent?' asked Ebenezer, his voice shaking a little, the grave attitude of this agent frightened him.

'Come, why so mysterious, surely you can tell me your name?'

Ebenezer was having trouble focusing on the man as his dark visage blended so well within the dark and gloom within his room.

The Agent raised his hand and pointed to the screen.

Ebenezer felt fear, true bone chilling, and spine tingling fear as he leaned forward to stare into the screen.

This man was death; he knew that within his soul. One of those Agents licensed to kill.

He wondered whether he was here to kill him.

A flicker on the screen captured his attention, and he felt the now familiar sensation of being drawn into the screen.

Ebenezer saw he was standing outside No 10, and the voices became clearer as he took in the scene.

'He's dead then?'

'Aye, they found him this morning.'

'Died in the night?'

'Aye, looks that way.'

'What did he die of?'

'I don't know, maybe his heart finally froze.'

'Well, not to speak ill of the dead but perhaps it's for the best.'

'Aye, we have a chance now for some real change.'

'When's the funeral?'

'In a few days, I suspect. I doubt there will be many that make the trip over to attend.'

'Cheap then, he'd have liked that.'

'Indeed he would've.'

The conversation seemed almost jovial to Ebenezer's ears, and he wondered who had died.

'They might even be looking for mourners to fill the pews.'

'Well, I don't mind going if there is a wake afterwards.'

Laughter followed this remark.

'You'll do anything for a free lunch.'

'I'll only go if you are going; otherwise I'll not bother. It's not as if he did me any good.'

'Time I was off. Let's see if we can save what's left of our term in office for I cannot see us getting another four years.'

The group broke up and went their separate ways.

Ebenezer knew the men and women of course and looked to the Agent to explain what he was seeing.

The scene changed, and he was on a street now, watching as two men approached each other.

'Cold for the time of year.'

'Good for skating.'

'Not a skater myself.'

'The job is done then?'

'Indeed.'

'Detectable?'

'No.'

The two men parted.

Ebenezer struggled to decode the mystery of these conversations.

Someone had died that was clear. But who?

Everything the other two agents had shown him had made him who he had become; how his actions affected others, and he believed this third agent would be no different, so this death was important.

Perhaps it was a key political figure? A Head of State? Perhaps the leader of the Opposition?

Ebenezer chuckled to himself. *That would be too much to hope for*, he thought, and then chided himself for thinking such a thing.

He had hoped he would see predictions of wealth and prosperity amongst the poorer quarters, of changes to the policies he was thinking of making. But, of course, the Agent wouldn't have known that. No, the Agent will show him the future results of his current policies.

Ebenezer steeled himself for more harrowing scenes, comforted only that he planned to make changes.

Ebenezer was jerked from his thoughts as a shiver ran down his spine. He looked up from the screen. The Agent's face was shadowed as he stood back within the darkness; nevertheless, Ebenezer knew the man was looking directly at him, and he felt another shiver run down his spine.

The screen flickered and drew his attention though he would rather not look. Nevertheless, he leaned in and focused on the images that lay before him.

He recognised the streets only by the fact they were ones he would never enter. The Poor Quarter. That area of the city hardest hit by the reforms. An area of dirt and grime. The streets ran dark with filth, the houses, and shops dishevelled and in need of repair. Crime was rife within the Quarter, the strongest taking from the weakest what little they had to survive, the weakest dying, often alone in some alley or backroom somewhere, days, sometimes weeks passing before they were reported and carted off.

In truth, the only thing that prospered in the Poor Quarter was the rats. As big as cats and just as fearless.

There was one shop in the Poor Quarter that everyone knew; that everyone visited at sometime or other; The Duck and Drake, the pawnbrokers.

The pawnbroker bought anything and everything for there was money to be made if you knew who valued which items. From metals to textiles, glass to crockery, toys to books, everything had value.

The broker was an old fellow. Spending his days sitting by a barbecue burner, filled with charcoal that glowed a deep red, smoking a pipe. What little hair he had, hung in greasy grey tangles down to his shoulders. His glasses were cracked and smudged upon his nose and he wore gloves without fingers upon his hands.

A bell jangled announcing someone had entered the shop, and Ebenezer turned to see a woman walking up the narrow aisle between the shopkeeper's wares, a large bag flung over one shoulder.

The bell jangled again and he saw not one but two people walking up the aisle. Another woman, also carrying a bundle over one shoulder, and a man, unburdened.

The three visitors and the pawnbroker regarded each other for one moment then the tension broke, laughter burst forth, and handshakes were given and taken all around.

'Agent, who are these three, are they part of my future in some way?' asked Ebenezer

The Agent just looked at Ebenezer and then back to the scene as the first woman spoke.

'Cold for the time of year,' said the first woman.

'Good for skating,' said the man.

'Not a skater myself,' said the second woman.

'Come on through to the back,' invited the pawnbroker. 'Wait one moment whilst I shut up the shop.'

As the door closed, it screeched on its rusty hinges.

'Wow, Catesby, put some oil on those will you?' said the man.

'Na, goes with the shop. A good cover is all about the details,' replied the pawnbroker.

They all moved through the door at the back and into a much more pleasant room.

'Welcome to my parlour,' Catesby said. 'Report.'

'Are we not waiting for the others?' asked the woman.

'No, I have their reports,' said Catesby.

'Let me go first then,' said the second woman.

'And then me,' said the first woman.

'Aye and I will go last,' said the man.

'I was able to secure the job as Housekeeper when the other woman left, and I also leased the cellar that lay directly under his house with no problems,' said the second woman.

'I started the laundry service in that cellar as planned and even took to cleaning his sheets and linens,' said the first woman.

Catesby nodded and looked at the man expectantly.

'And you, Guy?'

'The fire went through the house as expected, leaving no evidence of arson. And I have the contract to take his body from the house to his grave,' said Guy. 'No one cares to examine the body further.'

'Any problems, Ms Percy?' the shopkeeper asked.

'Not a one,' said the housekeeper. 'He was such a curmudgeon no one cared to stay with him any longer than they had to. So he was alone at the last.'

'If he was a little kinder we would not have had to come together as we have,' said Guy.

'Perhaps,' said Catesby, 'perhaps. It was a judgement call and a tough one at that.'

'Well, I for one, thought it was a judgement that would weigh heavier than it does,' said the laundress.

'I agree, Ms Wright, taking a life should weigh heavier but in this case....... A sign, perhaps, that it was indeed necessary and just, and not a sin?'

Catesby remained silent, regarding each of the three co-conspirators before rubbing his hands together.

'So, what have you brought me?'

'Well, I've brought most of his linens with me. Figured you could sell 'em in your shop,' said Ms Wright, pushing her bundle into the middle of the group, fumbling with the knot, untying it.

'And I,' said Guy, 'have these.'

Catesby looked at Ms Wright, then shrugged and took the wares off Guy.

'A pair of cufflinks, nice, nice. A pocket watch? Not worth much I'm afraid, and what's this? A pencil case? Ummm not bad, could sell that,' mumbled Catesby under his breath, as he sorted through the bits.

Catesby sorted through some coins, picking out some, dropping one back into the tin, selecting another, and added a single note. He gazed at the selection, nodded, and then handed them to Guy.

'Not one coin more, so don't be asking.'

Ms Wright was next. Pulling out sheets, towels, some clothes, as expected. Then hidden amongst the linens she produced some silver teaspoons and sugar tongs, placing them down with some ceremony.

'Nice, very nice,' said Catesby. He picked out a couple of notes and added some more coins, mumbling under his breath though loud enough for everyone to hear. 'Too soft, Catesby, too soft by half, you are weak when it comes to the ladies though they scarcely give you a second look.'

Turning he placed the money into the outstretched hand.

'And now for my bundle,' said Ms Percy, dropping her bundle down and undoing the ties.

'What are these, curtains?' said Catesby.

'Yes, his curtains, his bed curtains no less.'

'How did you manage to get his bed curtains?' asked Ms Wright. 'Surely you didn't take 'em with him asleep in his bed.'

Ms Percy nodded.

'I slipped him something to make him sleep deep. A Christen service as I see it, so he wouldn't feel anything when he cooked, so why not take a little something in return?'

'Blankets, you took his blankets too?' said Catesby, pulling them out of the bundle.

'Well, figured he would be warm soon enough,' she said with a chuckle.

Ebenezer was stunned by such callousness as they pawed over the pilfered belongings of a dead man. A man dead by their own hands no less.

'Agent, I can see why you would show me this. It's a warning, am I right? That I too may end up like this unfortunate man?'

The scene changed, and Ebenezer looked upon a four poster bed upon which lay a body covered by a single sheet.

Ebenezer thought he could smell the smoke he could see creeping under the door and feel the heat coming up through the floorboards.

'Who lays here?' he asked aloud.

The body moved slightly, restlessly, though the cover moved only a fraction, not enough to slip from the face and reveal itself.

'Is there no one who will mourn this man's passing?'

The scene changed, and Ebenezer leaned in hopefully, seeking a glimmer of light in such a dark night.

A woman was pacing within a room; her constant glances at the door suggesting she was expecting someone, someone important to her as she could barely keep still and she snapped at the children to be quiet.

The door opened, and a man entered, his face creased in worry, tension, and relief?

Ebenezer puzzled over the expression as he watched the man take a seat at the table.

'Thomas Wintour, tell me this instant, what has happened?'

Thomas looked at his wife. 'He's dead.'

'Oh thank God,' she said. 'May I be forgiven for saying so. Who will be his successor do you think?'

'I don't know, but surely whoever he or she is, it couldn't be worse.'

'I know it is awful, but I feel like dancing,' the woman said, and a small giggle escaped before she placed her hands, one covering the other, over her mouth.

'Caroline,' said Thomas gravely, though Ebenezer could see a smile tugging at his lips.

He rose and held out his hands in which Caroline placed hers.

The kids were by the door, listening in. 'Is it good news or bad?' one whispered.

'I'm not sure, one moment it seems bad the next good.'

Their doubts were dispelled when they saw their Dad whirl their Mum around and then dance and jig.

Ebenezer looked at the Agent.

'Truly? There is no one who is in the least bit sorry for the loss of the man? Was he truly so wretched and grim that all are glad of his death?'

The scene changed.

CHAPTER TEN

DEATH

'Why, it's Cratchit's house,' said Ebenezer in surprise. 'Oh no, was it a relation of his? His father? His father-in-law?'

Everyone was quiet and sombre in the house and Ebenezer was drawn into the scene.

Peter was reading a story to the younger children, whilst Mrs Cratchit and her two older daughters were sawing at the table.

The mother laid down her work, rubbing her eyes.

'My eyes are not what they used to be,' she said. 'Besides your father will be home soon.'

'He comes home later and later these days,' said Peter.

The mother nodded. 'Since Tim died, he walks much slower,' she said. 'No longer a steed to carry Tim at a gallop.'

'Oh, Tim so used to love that,' said Peter.

'I can still hear his laughter and screeching as Dad would go faster and faster, and Tim would bounce so on his shoulders,' said Mother, her voice catching at the end.

'Here he is,' cried Martha, getting up from the table.

Bel and the others all stood expectantly as their Dad walked into the room.

Ebenezer could see the light had gone out in Bob Cratchit; his eyes had lost their sparkle, his step its bounce.

'Come, sit by the fire, Bob. We saved you your tea.'

The two young twins, one boy, one girl, each climbed up and sat on a leg each, their little arms combining to circle his waist and hug him.

'Don't be sad. Tim is in heaven looking down and happier for it,' said the boy.

'We miss him too, but if we keep him in our hearts he's still with us,' said the little girl.

Ebenezer tried to swallow the grief that swelled up within him as he watched such a heart-wrenching scene.

'I know little ones. I know. I do try, honest I do.' He hugged them both to him as he saw the work the girls had been doing.

'You three have been working so hard on his robes,' he said. 'I can see they will be ready for Sunday.'

'You went to the grave site today?' asked Mrs Cratchit.

Bob nodded. 'Don't be angry with me. I know I said I would wait until we all go Sunday, but I had to see, had to make sure..........'

Bob let out a sob, followed by another and another. Once started he couldn't seem to stop.

'My poor little boy, I miss him so much.'

Mrs Cratchit took his head to her breast and held him as he cried and cried.

After a long while, he pulled his head away and sniffed.

'Sorry,' he said. 'I'll be just a moment,' and went upstairs.

There on the bed was Tim, lying so still and so peaceful.

Bob took the seat next to him and held his hand.

He noticed someone had decorated the room with Christmas decorations, and it gladdened his heart, as Tim did love Christmas so.

'Hello, my boy, my dear, Tim. Mum and your sisters are working so hard on your robes, and I saw your gra.... resting place today, and it looks so nice and quiet. We will visit so often you will hardly miss us at all, and I'll tell you everything that is going on, all that we are doing.'

Despite the tears rolling down his cheeks, Bob managed to keep his voice steady and light, for Tim's sake.

'I think of you every day, you know, carrying you on my shoulders, we had such fun. I will carry you in my heart, my lad and remember you, always.'

Ebenezer cried openly as he listened to Bob talking to his son.

Bob sat silently now, never letting go of Tim's hand.

He looked up, when he felt a hand on his shoulder, to see his wife, tears in her eyes, looking down on their son and he patted it and gave it a squeeze.

Behind her were the others, all standing quietly.

Bob stood up, feeling at peace and smiled at his wife. He smiled at his children and shooed them all downstairs. Bob was the last to leave but before he did, he placed his forehead against Tim's and whispered, 'I miss you so very much,' kissed his bald head as he always had and followed the others downstairs.

Bob stood in the room downstairs, looking, and feeling calmer.

He took his wife into his arms and held her.

'You are such a good wife,' he said.

'Come sit, tell us about your day as you eat,' she said.

Bob sat and sipped the thin soup off his spoon.

'I met Fred today, Mr Scrooge's nephew, well he saw me really and asked what was wrong, and I told him about...... everything, and he was really very kind. He gave me his card and said to call him if there was anything he could do.'

'That was very kind of him,' said Mrs Cratchit.

'I thought so too,' said Bob.

'He even mentioned about finding some work for Peter.'

'He never did? Really? Do you think he will?' asked Mrs Cratchit.

'I think he will, otherwise why mention it?' said Bob.

'Then Peter can finally propose to his girlfriend,' teased Martha.

'Leave off,' said Peter laughing, 'we've only been dating a year.'

Ebenezer blinked as he realised he was in his own bedroom and not within the Cratchit household.

'Agent, I can feel time is growing short, and I must know. Who was that man who lay in that bed?'

Ebenezer could feel the eyes of the Agent upon him though he could scarcely make him out, so enshrouded by the dark.

He did see the pale white hand with its skeletal thin finger point to the screen.

Ebenezer looked to see a new scene appear, one that filled him with foreboding and dread.

The scene was familiar to him as it was his office yet it was different. Someone had changed the furniture, and there, behind the desk, sat Matthews, the cheek of the man.

'Jump in my grave as quick,' Ebenezer scoffed.

The scene changed, and he stood before an iron gate.

He watched, as it swung open.

Ebenezer found himself in a graveyard. The clouds were dark and ominous, heralding rain. The cawing of crows seemed apt for such a place as grating their sound was to him.

'At least the mystery of that poor dead soul will be laid to rest,' said Ebenezer to the Agent.

The Agent just pointed.

Ebenezer grunted.

'Ok, no need to shout,' he grumbled under his breath, and moved amongst the gravestones.

The graveyard in the main was well kept, neat, and pleasant to visit one's departed. Ebenezer looked back at the Agent whose hand still pointed and followed the direction as best he could.

He looks right at home here, he thought, as he stumbled over a loose stone laid flat on the ground.

He noticed this area was unkempt, the grass longer, weeds aplenty, the graves themselves long since abandoned to the elements, neglected and unloved.

The very air here smelt of death and decay. Not to wonder, as the gardener kept his compost close by, heaped up against the brick wall at the rear of the graveyard.

Ebenezer was startled to find the Agent suddenly in front of him pointing down to one grave.

'Before I look, for fear of what I will find, tell me, where the first Agent showed me things of my past, and the second of the present day, do you show me what *may* happen, Agent, what *may* come to pass? If I change my policies, change my very nature, and then these things will not be so? If I can change the course of a river, then I must also be able to change its destination, is that not so, Agent?'

The Agent was as silent as ever.

Ebenezer took one step forward, then another, as if creeping up on the gravestone might somehow change what he feared to see.

The stone lay flat, though once it had stood upright. It was cracked and chipped, greyed and broken off from its base.

On the flat surface was a simple inscription:

EBENEZER SCROOGE

Ebenezer dropped to his knees as he read his own name upon the gravestone.

He scrubbed at the lichen and grime that marked and stained it, tears upon his face.

Suddenly a thought struck him.

'Agent, was that me on the bed covered in but a single sheet?

Was I the man they were talking about in the Duck and Drake?

Was I left to burn *alive* whilst they took my things?'

The Agent simply pointed to the grave and then back to Ebenezer.

'Marley said this was a warning. Surely, a warning means it's not too late to change, to alter my fate. I am not the man I was, I've changed, I can feel the change within me.'

Though nothing outwardly changed in the Agent's stance nor did he speak, but something within him softened, and Ebenezer sensed it.

'Agent, I can feel that you believe me, feel that you know I speak the truth, can you not give me any sign that I can alter this fate to another? If not for me, then for the country I love and the people I serve?'

The Agent lowered his hand.

'I will honour Christmas in my heart, not just once a year but all year and all the years to come. I will remember the lessons shown to me by Chris Ast and Chris Resent and you Agent though I do not know your name. I will not forget what I have seen these nights; I will make changes, changes for the betterment of all humankind. I promise this. I promise.'

Ebenezer realised the Agent had gone; the darkness had swallowed him whole.

He got to his feet, his body trembling and cried out, 'I will embody my Past, Present, and Future, Jacob, hear me, and may it gladden your heart and lighten your load.'

CHAPTER ELEVEN

THE MORNING

Ebenezer turned and looked around his room. He saw the bed curtains still hanging, his pocket watch still on the dresser where he had left it, his good shirt still hung in the wardrobe.

The future is not preordained. I can alter my course and change my destiny, he thought.

Ebenezer felt a lightness of spirit and a spring in his step. He felt so light he might float and leapt in the air to test the thought and landed with a thump.

Laughing aloud at his own silliness, he hopped and skipped around the room before realising he was still in his nightgown, his hat still upon his head.

He snatched it off, threw it down, pulled his nightgown up and over his head, and threw that away too.

Grabbing his clothes, he put his left foot into the right leg of his trousers, and his right arm into the left sleeve of his shirt, but never said a cross word or curse about it. He just laughed and cried and laughed some more.

'Merry Christmas and a Happy New Year,' he said to his reflection in the mirror.

'Happy Christmas and a Merry New Year,' he shouted out as he spun around trying to get his arm into his jacket.

He had to stop, as he felt dizzy. The room spun a little longer as he wobbled on his feet, breathing deeply.

'Oh, wow, not as young as I once was,' he said aloud.

He opened his door, and walked through his sitting room humming to himself. Opening the sitting room door, he looked into the hall.

'Cratchit, where are you man?' he called.

'I wonder what day it is?' he said aloud, and then laughed. 'What a silly old sod, not knowing what day it is.'

For someone who had not laughed much in his lifetime and certainly not for many, many years, his laugh was a wonderful one, full of vigour and joy.

Indeed, the boy that came running up the stairs and along the passage to see who was laughing, had a smile as broad as broad could be, to hear such a laugh. He could not believe his eyes when he saw the source of such merriment.

'Mum sent me to see if you needed anything, Sir.'

'Need anything? Need anything? Why; I do have need young man. Can you tell me what day it is?'

'The day, Sir?'

'Yes, the day, Sir, if you please?'

'It's Christmas Day, Sir.'

'Christmas Day. Christmas Day?' he muttered to himself. 'How could that be?'

He tottered up on his fingers the three visits and the clock striking and looked at his fingers and then at the boy.

'Christmas Day you say? I haven't missed it?'

'No, Sir, it is Christmas Day,' the boy said. 'All day,' he added.

'All day indeed,' repeated Ebenezer, laughing aloud.

The Agents came and went within one night, he thought, *that must be it. The wonder of it.*

He pondered it no more; he had too many things to do. So many he didn't know where to start.

'Young man, you said your Mother sent you. Who prey is your Mother?'

'Mrs Poulter, the housekeeper, Sir.'

'The Housekeeper? The housekeeper! Yes, yes. Tell me, young man, is the turkey still hanging in the larder?'

'The one as big as me, Sir? Yes, Sir, it's still there. Mum says you won't let us cook it so she's going to give it back tomorrow.'

'Well, you run and tell her to do no such thing. Tell her to cook......, no, no, *ask* her if she would be so good as to cook it for Christmas Dinner and *ask* her if she and your good self would like to join me.'

'Really, Sir? We can join you for Christmas Dinner, and we're going to have turkey?'

'Indeed, boy, indeed. Turkey and all the trimmings as many as your Mum is willing to make.'

The boy jumped up and down, his tummy already rumbling in anticipation.

'Run along, young man, run along.'

The boy raced off yelling, 'Mum! Mum!'

'What a pleasant boy, lovely lad,' said Ebenezer to no one, no one at all.

Ebenezer walked to his office, bidding 'Good Morning' and 'Merry Christmas' to his security detail, the two men patrolling the house. 'Dinner will be at 3pm, gentlemen, do say you will join me?'

The guards were surprised, shocked would be a more fitting word but happy to accept. Both single, and without family, they had drawn Christmas duty, and it had promised to be a dull affair, but not now. The prospect of a turkey roast and all the trimmings had their mouth's watering.

Ebenezer took his seat behind the desk. *His* seat behind *his* desk and laughed as he realised it to be so.

Picking up the phone, he pressed one and waited.

'Cratchit Household,' came a young voice.

'Hello, young lady, may I speak to your father please?'

Ebenezer had to push the phone away from his ear as the young girl screamed out, 'DAAAAAAAAAAAAD! PHONNNNE!'

'I DON'T KNOW!'

'Hello? Who is it please?'

'Tell him it's Prime Minister Scrooge.'

'HE SAYS HE'S THE PRIME MINISTER!'

'Hello, Sir, Hello? Is everything all right?'

'Bob? Bob, its Ebenezer. Everything's fine I was just wondering if you would be so kind to join me for Christmas dinner, you, and all your family?'

'Err, Yes, Sir that would be lovely, Sir. Thank you. Are you quite sure everything is all right?'

'Yes Yes, Bob, everything is fine.'

'Ok, Sir, Christmas dinner would be lovely. What time should we arrive?'

'Errrrr, yes, well you see, I've kind of sprung this on the housekeeper last minute so if you could all come over as soon as possible, I was thinking, perhaps, maybe, that is, could Mrs Cratchit lend her a hand? I would of course, but I don't know the first thing about cooking.'

'Yes, Sir, of course, Sir, she would be delighted to help, Sir. And, you are quite all right, Sir? Feeling ok?'

'I am fine, Bob, better than fine. Oh and, Bob, you will have tomorrow off as well, to spend with your family, paid of course, and a bonus, a Christmas Bonus and a pay rise, and and.....'

Ebenezer didn't know how else to start making amends with Bob, his mind was in a whirl.

'Oh and medical benefit included, for you and your family.'

'Medical, really? Wow, my God, that's so generous of you, Sir, thank you.'

'Don't say another word, Bob, not generous not by a half of it. Long overdue but I will make amends, Bob, I promise I will make amends.'

'....... ok.... Yes, Sir......... I am not sure what to say, Sir.'

'Merry Christmas, Bob. I'll see you when you all get here.'

'Merry Christmas to you too, Sir.'

Ebenezer hung on and then dialled another number.

'Fred, my boy, my lad. Merry Christmas to you and your good wife.'

'Errrr, Merry Christmas to you to, Uncle? Are you quite all right, are you feeling ok?'

Ebenezer laughed aloud.

'Why does everyone keep asking me that? I am better than all right my lad, my fine boy, I am reborn. I phoned to say I cannot make it to dinner today as I am having people over but if the invitation extends to tomorrow I would be honoured by your hospitality.'

'Of course, Uncle, you are always welcome. You have made my Christmas, honestly you have.'

Ebenezer felt a lump in his throat.

'Well and good then, I will see you tomorrow, lots to do, so much to do.'

'Yes, Uncle and a Merry Christmas to you. We'll see you tomorrow.'

'Merry Christmas, my boy, Merry Christmas!'

Ebenezer placed the phone back in its cradle. He heard footsteps outside his office and went seeking their owner, not expecting anyone in the building today, being Christmas and all.

'Mr Matthews what are you doing here?' Ebenezer asked, as he spied the portly figure of his Minister for Housing.

'Sir, I'm sorry if I disturbed you. I'm just trying to arrange some accommodation for a family in dire need.'

'No disturbance, Sir. Tell me, do you still have those plans you drew up to improve the housing for all such families in desperate need?'

'I do, Sir.'

'And, if you had the funds, you could implement these changes immediately?'

'Yes, Sir, this very day in fact. I have a list of families I could house within Bed and Breakfast establishments until proper housing was available, Sir.'

'Then do so, Mr Matthews, do so. Take this.' Ebenezer held out his credit card, 'and put that family you mentioned up in a hotel until you can find them proper accommodation. Then be off home with you. You have a wife and two children if I'm not mistaken, and Christmas is for family.'

'Yes, Sir, I will get on it right away and be off home immediately thereafter.'

'Good man. One more thing, Mr Matthews.'

'Yes, Sir?'

'I would like you to record the Christmas Message to the nation, tell them about the changes to Housing you are proposing.'

'Me, Sir? Surely, you should make those announcements, Sir. They will be well received and will see you through to a second term.'

'That might be so, Mr Matthews, but I don't deserve the credit for those changes, you do and I would like the nation to know that too. Who knows, one day you could be sitting in my chair.'

'Yes, Sir, I mean no, Sir, I mean in time maybe, Sir.'

Ebenezer roared with laughter.

'Indeed, Sir, in time. Is Mr Brown in his office as well?'

'Yes, Sir, actually, Sir, he's standing behind you.'

Ebenezer turned to see Mr Brown standing in the doorway of his office, staring in amazement, the sound of laughter having drawn him from his chair.

'Mr Brown, do you still have your plans for the employment opportunities for the poorer quarters, closing the Reclamation Yards and increasing the wages and improving the conditions for the factories and workhouses?'

'Yes, Sir I do.'

'Excellent, join Mr Matthews and include those changes in the Christmas Message and then be off home with you, enjoy Christmas and I don't want to see either of you tomorrow. Take the whole day off, you both deserve it.'

'Yes, Sir, Thank you, Sir.'

'Oh and, gentlemen.'

'Yes, Sir?'

'MERRY CHRISTMAS to you both.'

'A Merry Christmas to you, Sir.'

'Merry Christmas, Mr Prime Minister.'

Ebenezer grabbed his coat and headed for the door.

'Sir, wait one moment please.'

His two security agents grabbed their coats and hurried to his side.

'Come on, lads; we're going shopping.'

*

Ebenezer was reasonably well known, so when he hammered on the toyshop window repeatedly, the shopkeeper was first shocked and then extremely happy to let Ebenezer in as he bought so much he and his guards could scarcely carry it all. But carry it all they did.

*

Ebenezer surveyed the piles of toys and the rolls of wrapping paper.

'Any good at wrapping presents?' he said to his agents.

'Not bad, Sir,' said one, slipping off his jacket and, kneeling on the carpet, got cracking with the wrapping.

Ebenezer and the other agent were quick to follow and before long, the presents were wrapped and piled high.

'Tell me, have you ever heard of a Chris Ast?' Ebenezer asked conversationally.

'Agent Ast, yes of course. He's in the photo on the wall outside your office.'

'He is?' said Ebenezer in surprise and got up to take a look.

There, on the wall was a photo of three agents standing together outside No.10.

Reading the inscription underneath it read:

Mr Chris P Ast, Chris P Resent and Chris F Uture.

Died in the line of duty 2015.

Ebenezer felt the ground shift beneath his feet, and he placed his hand on the wall to steady himself.

There were the three agents staring out at him from the photo.

They died? Seven years ago?

Ebenezer stared at the photo silently for the longest time before he tapped the glass and said, 'I will remember my lessons gentlemen, I promise you that.'

Ebenezer walked into his office and spying his favourite mints in a dish cried out with pleasure,

'HUMBUG!'

EPILOGUE

Ebenezer was true to his word and more.

The Housing and Employment bills went through without a hitch, and their implementation was immediate and far reaching.

More Foreign Aid was sent out, Welfare, Infrastructure, Health, and Education were all given huge budgets to right the wrongs of the Welfare and Reforms Policies Prime Minister Marley, and he had introduced.

Bob Cratchit received all he was promised and more as the increases to his salary were backdated by seven years and Tim received all the medical care he needed and did not die. Indeed, Ebenezer Scrooge became a firm family friend to the Cratchit's who were always delighted to see him whenever he visited.

He gained a second term in office and became one of the most revered leaders in history. His manner was one of such honesty and openness, his laugh so easy to come by, everyone loved him and couldn't keep the smiles off their faces. Something that vexed the opposition party who gave up trying to bait the Prime Minister during the debates and got down to some real governing, asking real questions and responding with real answers. The face of politics had changed with Ebenezer Scrooge and changed for the better.

And, as for Christmas, never was it said that Ebenezer Scrooge didn't know how to celebrate Christmas, nor did he save it for just once a year, often calling out 'CHRISTMAS!' whenever he heard or saw something that reminded him of that festive time of year.

Therefore, I will end this tale with perhaps the most immortal of phrases;

God Bless us. Every One!

Contact

http://simonhartwell.blogspot.co.uk/

simonhartwell @rocketmail.com

32102380R00085

Printed in Poland
by Amazon Fulfillment
Poland Sp. z o.o., Wrocław